Shirley's Cakes

FRESHLY BAKED BY

Ambur Lowenthal
& Joe Werner

Schiffer Books are available at special discounts for bulk purchases for sales promotions or premiums. Special editions, including personalized covers, corporate imprints, and excerpts can be created in large quantities for special needs. For more information contact the publisher:

Published by Schiffer Publishing Ltd.
4880 Lower Valley Road
Atglen, PA 19310
Phone: (610) 593-1777; Fax: (610) 593-2002
E-mail: Info@schifferbooks.com

For the largest selection of fine reference books on this and related subjects,please visit our website at: www.schifferbooks.com. We are always looking for people to write books on new and related subjects. If you have an idea for a book, please contact us at proposals@schifferbooks.com

This book may be purchased from the publisher.
Include $5.00 for shipping.
Please try your bookstore first.

You may write for a free catalog.

In Europe, Schiffer books are distributed by
Bushwood Books
6 Marksbury Ave.
Kew Gardens
Surrey TW9 4JF England
Phone: 44 (0) 20 8392 8585; Fax: 44 (0) 20 8392 9876
E-mail: info@bushwoodbooks.co.uk
Website: www.bushwoodbooks.co.uk

Shirley hated cake. That's right. CAKE. She hated the frosting, the sweet sugar smell, the crumbs, and the way it made her mouth dry.

She hated birthday cake, especially the pink and yellow frosting balloons.

"Frosting's bitter!" She'd exclaim after running her fingers through the sugary goo.

She hated holiday cakes:

"That doesn't look like a Christmas Tree!"

"Rabbits aren't fat! NOR do they lay eggs!"

Good Job, Columbus!

"Columbus didn't discover America, the Vikings did! This cake is a historical fallacy!"

Shirley's hatred of all imaginable cakes soon got on the nerves of her friends and family, especially after she lodged a complaint about her little brother's 'First Day of School Cake.'

WHERE'S THE BUS DRIVER?

SCHOOL

"Baby girl," her mother began, "the frosting is merely an interpretation of what a school bus looks like."

"I like realism in my cake, Mother," replied Shirley.

Her mother sighed, "But you hate cake."

Shirley furrowed her brow, "Exactly."

"Shirley, I love cacti! They're what I want on my birthday cake!" exclaimed Greta, Shirley's best friend. Her birthday was fast-approaching.

GEOGRAPHICALLY AND BOTANICALLY INACCURATE!

Happy Birthday, Greta!

"Um, we live in Michigan. Cacti are not indigenous to our ecosystem!" Shirley replied, adding, "You want a cacti, move to Nevada!"

Greta cried, "But... we're best friends!"

"Are we, Greta? Are we?"

9

Even at the annual field trip to the Rolling Pin Bakery, Shirley was causing a raucous.

"Excuse me, Ms. Baker, why would you bake? Why not have a real job! You could be a doctor and help people," said Shirley.

The baker replied, "I make cakes to help people celebrate wonderful times. I share my best talent with the people around me. What do you do Shirley?"

Shirley stood stunned.

"Shirley," her teacher gently said, "maybe you should sit outside so we can talk?"

"It's not fair!" Shirley cried out, "Why am I in trouble because I think cake is dumb?"

"I'm not upset that you don't like cake, everyone accepts that about you," her teacher replied, "I'm upset that you don't accept the life choices of others."

At that moment, Shirley realized how she had been acting.

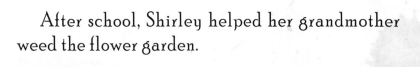

After school, Shirley helped her grandmother weed the flower garden.

"I heard what happened at school today," her grandmother said, "Shirley, if you hate cake so much don't eat it! No one is forcing cake in your mouth!"

"But Grandma, maybe one day, one marvelous day, I'll find a cake that is perfect! From taste, to frosting, and right down to the perfect occasion!" said Shirley.

"Well, you might have to make that cake yourself!" her grandmother replied.

12

A light bulb went on.

Then a spotlight.

THEN a star supernovaed in a far off galaxy! Shirley knew what she had to do!

She ran into the kitchen
and began tearing through
the cabinets. She grabbed
flour, sugar, vanilla, chocolate,
eggs, and butter. Then she
found the measuring cups,
spoons, bowls, and a pan to
bake the batter.

She mixed. She smelled. She tasted the batter until she thought it was perfect. Into the oven the pan went.

While it baked, she began mixing the frosting: butter, powdered sugar, cream cheese, and orange zest. She mixed until it was smooth and creamy!

Then she took the cake out of the oven and paced the kitchen while it cooled.

By this time her family noticed what she was doing and gathered to watch.

Her little brother ran to tell the neighborhood kids, and they all came and peered in through the kitchen window. They all watched as she slathered frosting on the cooled cake.

It looked simple. No pine trees, no cacti, no Columbus... Just cake and frosting.

"Perfect," she whispered.

Everyone's mouths were watering at the scent. Shirley cut
the cake and passed out a slice for everyone.

The room was silent as they waited for her to take the first bite. Shirley held the dish and fork. She took a deep breath and then dug her fork into the moist cake and took the first bite.

Her eyes closed. "Yum!" She murmured, mouth full of cake.

Everyone ate and loved her cake!

From that day forward Shirley made everyone's cakes.

Shirley's Shazam Chocolate Cake

INGREDIENTS:

1 cup butter

1 cup boiling water

1/4 cup cocoa

2 cups sugar

2 cups flour

1/8 teaspoon salt

2 whole eggs

1 teaspoon baking soda

1/2 cup sour cream

1 teaspoon vanilla

STEP 1) In a large sauce pan, combine the butter, water and cocoa over medium heat. Heat the mixture until the butter melts.

1 cup butter

1 cup boiling water

1/4 cup cocoa

STEP 2) Add the sugar, flour, eggs, baking soda, sour cream, salt and vanilla. Mix well.

2 cups sugar

2 cups flour

1/8 teaspoon salt

2 whole eggs

1 teaspoon baking soda

1/2 cup sour cream

1 teaspoon vanilla

STEP 3) Wipe the bottom and sides of a 15"x10" pan with butter and then sprinkle with flour. Pour the batter into pan.

STEP 4) Bake at 350° for 15 to 20 minutes. Stick a toothpick in the center of the cake - it will come out clean if the cake is done.

Shirley's Outrageous Orange Frosting

INGREDIENTS:

1/2 cup butter at room temperature

8 oz cream cheese at room temperature

2 - 3 tablespoons fresh orange juice

the zest of one whole orange

2 - 3 cups powdered sugar

STEP 1) With an electric mixer, mix the cream cheese and butter together for about 3 minutes on medium speed until smooth. Scrape down the sides and bottom of the bowl to ensure even mixing.

1/2 cup butter

8 oz cream cheese

STEP 2) Zest a whole, large, plump orange using a grater or citrus zester into the mixture. Squeeze the juice out of the orange. Measure out the juice and add to the bowl. Mix well.

the zest of one whole orange

2 - 3 tablespoons orange juice

STEP 3) Slowly add the powdered sugar bit by bit, mixing as you go. Keep adding and mixing until you get to the desired sweetness and thickness.

2 - 3 cups powdered sugar

STEP 4) Spread the frosting on the cooled cake with a spatula or spoon into a piping bag to decorate your cake! Be sure to share your treat with family and friends!

27

CUPCAKE INGREDIENTS:

1 stick unsalted butter, softened
1 1/4 cups granulated sugar
the zest of 3 limes
2 large eggs at room temperature
--
1 3/4 cups flour
1 teaspoon baking powder
1/4 teaspoon baking soda
3/4 cup sour cream
the juice of three limes

1) Preheat oven to 350°F with rack in middle. Prepare your cupcake pan with your favorite cupcake liners.

2) Beat together butter, granulated sugar, and zest with an electric mixer until fluffy. Beat in eggs 1 at a time.

3) Combine the flour, baking powder and baking soda.

4) Stir together sour cream and fresh lime juice.

5) At low speed, mix flour and cream mixtures into egg mixture alternately in batches, beginning and ending with flour.

6) Spoon batter into cups and smooth top. Bake until golden and a wooden pick inserted into center comes out clean, 20 to 25 minutes. Let cool on a rack.

28

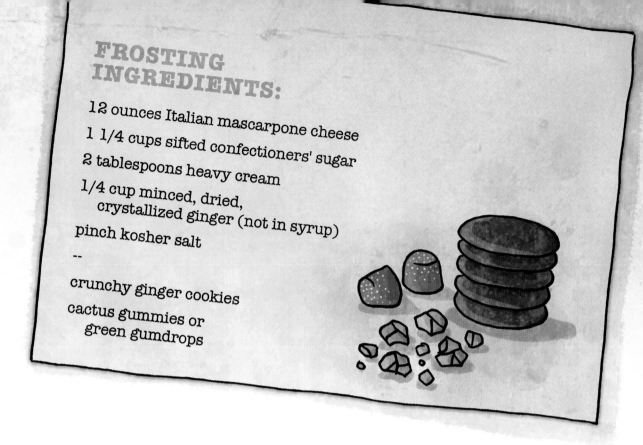

FROSTING INGREDIENTS:

12 ounces Italian mascarpone cheese

1 1/4 cups sifted confectioners' sugar

2 tablespoons heavy cream

1/4 cup minced, dried, crystallized ginger (not in syrup)

pinch kosher salt

--

crunchy ginger cookies

cactus gummies or green gumdrops

1) With an electric mixer, beat the mascarpone, confectioners' sugar, and cream together for about a minute, until light and fluffy.

2) Stir in the crystallized ginger and salt.

3) Frost the cupcakes.

4) Crush 16 ginger cookies until they resemble sand. Do this by putting them in a plastic bag and crushing them with a rolling pin or using a food processor.

5) Place the "sand" in a shallow bowl. Take a frosted cupcake, roll it in the "sand" and then top with your favorite cactus gummy!

Susan's Sweet Butter Cake

CAKE INGREDIENTS:

1 cup soft butter

2 cups sugar

4 eggs at room temperature

2 teaspoons vanilla

3 cups flour

1 teaspoon baking powder

1 teaspoon salt

1/2 teaspoon baking soda

1 cup buttermilk

SAUCE INGREDIENTS:

1 cup sugar

1/2 cup butter

1/4 cup water

1 tablespoon vanilla

From the Kitchen of
Susan Drews Watkins

Cake Instructions:

1) Preheat the oven to 350. Cream together butter and sugar with an electric mixer.

2) Add the eggs one at a time, mixing them in well.

3) Mix in the vanilla.

4) In a separate bowl, sift together flour, baking powder, salt, and baking soda.

5) Alternate mixing in flour mixture and buttermilk to the sugar/egg mixture.

6) Pour into greased and floured 10" tube or bundt pan.

7) Bake at 350 degrees for 70 minutes.

Sauce Instructions:

Add to cake while sauce is warm and cake has cooled a bit but still warm in pan.

1) Heat the sugar, butter and water in sauce pan until butter is melted and sugar dissolves - DO NOT let it come to a boil.

2) After the sugar has dissolved add the vanilla.

3) Let it cool down to warm (not cool), run a rubber spatula around sides of pan and prick the cake several times with a fork.

4) Pour sauce over the cake and down the sides of the pan. Use a rubber spatula to hold the cake away from pan so sauce runs to bottom.

5) Let it soak into cake and then flip cake out while still warmish.

About the Creators

Raised in the Great Plains of the American Midwest, Joe Werner and Ambur Lowenthal knew each other from sandboxes, corn fields and muskrat dens. Forged in the fire of make-believe and wonderment, they agreed to journey into a new world: storytelling. With their combined skills of artistry and word-smitherie, they will boldly traverse the universe of imagination to bring back all they have seen to you, our loving readers. To see what other tales Joe, Ambur and their friends have to tell, visit www.TheTreehouseCollective.com.